AFTER-SCHOOL SP⬤RTS CLUB

CLUB
Touchdown!

For Sparkles
—A. H.

For the kids and teachers at
Greentree Elementary School
—S. B.

SIMON SPOTLIGHT

An imprint of Simon & Schuster Children's Publishing Division
1230 Avenue of the Americas, New York, NY 10020
First Simon Spotlight paperback edition August 2010
Text copyright © 2010 by Simon & Schuster, Inc.
Illustrations copyright © 2010 by Steve Björkman
For information about special discounts for bulk purchases, please contact
Simon & Schuster Special Sales at 1-866-506-1949 or business@simonandschuster.com.
The Simon & Schuster Speakers Bureau can bring authors to your live event. For more
information or to book an event contact the Simon & Schuster Speakers Bureau at
1-866-248-3049 or visit our website at www.simonspeakers.com.
Designed by John Daly
The text of this book was set in Century Schoolbook BT.
The illustrations for this book were rendered in ink and watercolor.
Manufactured in the United States of America 0215 LAK
2 4 6 8 10 9 7 5 3
Library of Congress Cataloging-in-Publication Data
Heller, Alyson.
Touchdown! / written by Alyson Heller ; illustrated by Steve Björkman. — 1st Simon
Spotlight pbk. ed.
p. cm. — (After-School Sports Club) (Ready-to-read)
Summary: When the members of the After-School Sports Club play flag football, the
boys learn that girls can play football too.
ISBN 978-1-4169-9413-8
[1. Flag football—Fiction. 2. Sex role—Fiction. 3. Clubs—Fiction.] I. Björkman, Steve,
ill. II. Title.
PZ7.H374197To 2010
[E]—dc22
2009044212

AFTER-SCHOOL SPORTS CLUB
Touchdown!

Written by ALYSON HELLER

Illustrated by STEVE BJÖRKMAN

Ready-to-Read

Simon Spotlight
New York London Toronto Sydney New Delhi

One fall day Mr. Mac
and the kids gathered
on the field.

"We are going to play flag football," said Mr. Mac.

"But girls cannot play football," said J.B.

"Sure they can," said Mr. Mac.

"Yeah, J.B., they can play too!"
said Caleb.

The kids split into teams.

The first time down the field,
Alyssa lost her flag.

"I told you girls cannot play football!" said J.B.

Tess did not like that.

The next time down the field,
Tess took Caleb's flag.

"Go, Tess!" said Alyssa.

Then J.B. took Sammy's flag.

Soon just J.B. and Tess
were left on the field.

Tess was happy she was
still in the game.

On the next play Tess had the football. She ran to the left.

And ran to the right.

And ran right past J.B.
to make the touchdown!

"Woo-hoo!" everyone cheered—
except J.B.

"Nice job, Tess!" said Mr. Mac.

"See J.B., girls can play football!" Tess said. "Sorry I said girls could not play," said J.B.

"Do not worry. You can be on *my* team anytime!" Tess said.